Harold
the Helicopter

Based on *The Railway Series* **by the Rev. W. Awdry**

Illustrations by *Robin Davies*

EGMONT

EGMONT

We bring stories to life

First published in Great Britain 2005
This edition published in 2011
by Egmont UK Limited
The Yellow Building, 1 Nicholas Road, London W11 4AN

Thomas the Tank Engine & Friends™

CREATED BY BRITT ALLCROFT

Based on the Railway Series by the Reverend W Awdry
© 2011 Gullane (Thomas) LLC. A HIT Entertainment company.
Thomas the Tank Engine & Friends and Thomas & Friends are trademarks of Gullane (Thomas) Limited.
Thomas the Tank Engine & Friends and Design is Reg. U.S. Pat. & Tm. Off.

HiT entertainment

ISBN 978 1 4052 6968 1
43278/32
Printed in Italy

Stay safe online. Egmont is not responsible for content hosted by third parties.

FSC
MIX
Paper
FSC® C018306

Egmont is passionate about helping to preserve the world's remaining ancient forests.
We only use paper from legal and sustainable forest sources.

This book is made from paper certified by the Forest Stewardship Council® (FSC®),
an organisation dedicated to promoting responsible management of forest resources.
For more information on the FSC, please visit www.fsc.org. To learn more about
Egmont's sustainable paper policy, please visit www.egmont.co.uk/ethical

This is a story about Harold the Helicopter. He thought helicopters were faster than engines because they have propellers instead of wheels. But then Percy challenged him to a race . . .

Percy was delivering trucks of stone to the Harbour. At the Airfield nearby, there was a helicopter buzzing loudly as it waited to land.

"Loud, buzzy thing!" said Percy to his Driver. "I wish it would go and buzz somewhere else!"

The next day, Percy made a delivery to the Airfield. He stopped next to the helicopter.

"Hello," said Percy. "My name's Percy. Who are you?"

"I'm Harold," said the helicopter. "With my whirling propeller, I can fly like a bird! Don't you wish you had a propeller, too?"

"No, I like having my wheels on the rails," replied Percy, grumpily.

"You engines are much too slow," Harold continued. "With my propeller, I can go much faster than any of you!"

Percy was cross but before he could reply, Harold flew away.

Percy puffed angrily to the Quarry to pick up his next load of trucks.

"Hello, Percy," said Toby. "You look cross. What's the matter?"

Percy told Toby what Harold had said about helicopters being faster than engines.

"I'll show him he's wrong!" said Percy, firmly.

As Percy puffed back to the Harbour, he heard a familiar buzzing noise ahead of him.

"Look, Percy," said his Driver. "There's Harold. Let's race him! Then he'll see who's fastest!"

"Yes, we'll show him wheels are better than those funny whirling arms!" said Percy and he rushed after Harold.

Harold heard Percy speeding up behind him. He realised Percy was racing him to the Harbour.

"You'll never beat me!" he said, proudly. "I will have landed at the Airfield before you can stop at the Harbour Wharf!"

"Don't listen to him," said Percy's Driver. "We can win this!"

The race was on! Harold thought a little engine pulling heavy trucks full of stone could never beat him. But suddenly, he saw that Percy was drawing level with him.

A few minutes later Percy's Driver shouted, "We're in the lead, Percy!"

Percy was having the time of his life, racing along faster than he had ever gone before.

"Peep! Peep! Goodbye, Harold!" he shouted as he raced ahead.

Harold looked down in surprise. He couldn't believe Percy was beating him. Harold charged after him.

Percy's Fireman was shovelling coal into the furnace as fast as he could. He wiped a cloth across his hot face.

"Phew!" he said. "This is hard work. I hope we do beat Harold!"

Then he heard the signal that warned them the Harbour Wharf was nearby.

"Nearly there!" cried Percy's Driver. "I hope we've done enough to win!"

Percy braked as he approached the Wharf. He rolled under the main line and halted at the buffers, puffing loudly.

"Did . . . we . . . win?" he said breathlessly.

His Fireman scrambled on to the cab roof and looked at the Airfield. "We've won!" he gasped. "Harold's still looking for a place to land!"

Percy smiled. He had shown Harold that engines are just as fast as helicopters.

Later, Harold looked embarrassed when Percy made a delivery at the Airfield.

Percy's Driver and Fireman sang a song:
Said Harold Helicopter to our Percy,
"You are much too slow!
Your Railway is out of date
And not much use, you know."
But Percy with his stone trucks
Did the trip in record time,
And we beat Harold the Helicopter
On our Old Branch Line!

Harold smiled at Percy as he flew over him. "You showed me that you can go even faster than me," he said. "I guess wheels are as good as a propeller after all!"

Percy smiled happily. What fun it had been racing against Harold. He couldn't wait to get back to the engine shed and tell the others all about it.